Please return / renew by date shown.
You can renew it at:
norlink.norfolk.gov.uk
or by telephone: 0344 800 8006
Please have your library card & PIN ready

CAUCH

31/8/22

]

NORFOLK LIBRARY
AND INFORMATION SERVICE

NORFOLK ITEM

30129 057 467 376

Practising phonemes of more than one letter and
simple polysyllabic words + and / the / to / no / go

D0300139

First published in 2009 by
Franklin Watts
338 Euston Road
London NW1 3BH

Franklin Watts Australia
Hachette Children's Books
Level 17/207 Kent Street
Sydney NSW 2000

Text © Margaret Nash 2009
Illustration © Lisa Smith 2009

A CIP catalogue record for this book
is available from the British Library.

ISBN: 978 0 7496 9154 7 (hbk)
ISBN: 978 0 7496 9163 9 (pbk)

Series Editor: Jackie Hamley
Series Advisors: Dr Barrie Wade,
 Dr Hilary Minns
Series Designer: Jonathan Hair

Printed in China

Franklin Watts is a division of
Hachette Children's Books,
an Hachette UK company
www.hachette.co.uk

There is a puzzle at the end of this book.
Here are the answers for you to check later!

The matching words are:

Jess chess, less, mess

sock dock, lock, mock, shock

Bill chill, hill, mill, will

jacket packet

2

Bill put on his jacket.

But it did not fit.

The zip did not pull up.

"Put it in this sack, Bill."

6

"But, Dad ..."

"And that hat, Jess!
That can go in the sack."

"But, Dad ..."

"And the socks, Dad.
The socks can go in with
the hat."

"No, Jess! Not the socks!"

But Jess put the socks
in the sack.

"Yes, Dad. Buzz will have them."

Then Dad, Jess and Bill ran off to the shop.

17

Bill got a jacket.

Jess got a hat.

Dad got socks.

Buzz got a jacket, a hat and socks ...

and a kiss from Mum.

Puzzle Time!

Match the words that rhyme
to the pictures!

Jess

lock

chess

mill

sock

dock

chill

less

Bill

shock

mess

hill

packet

mock

will

jacket

See page 2 for answers!

Notes for parents and teachers

READING CORNER PHONICS has been structured to provide maximum support for children learning to read through synthetic phonics. The stories are designed for independent reading but may also be used by adults for sharing with young children.

The teaching of early reading through synthetic phonics focuses on the 44 sounds in the English language, and how these sounds correspond to their written form in the 26 letters of the alphabet. Carefully controlled vocabulary makes these books accessible for children at different stages of phonics teaching, progressing from simple CVC (consonant-vowel-consonant) words such as "top" (t-o-p) to trisyllabic words such as "messenger" (mess-en-ger). READING CORNER PHONICS allows children to read words in context, and also provides visual clues and repetition to further support their reading. These books will help develop the all important confidence in the new reader, and encourage a love of reading that will last a lifetime!

If you are reading this book with a child, here are a few tips:

1. Talk about the story before you start reading. Look at the cover and the title. What might the story be about? Why might the child like it?

2. Encourage the child to reread the story, and to retell the story in their own words, using the illustrations to remind them what has happened.

3. Discuss the story and see if the child can relate it to their own experience, or perhaps compare it to another story they know.

4. Give praise! Small mistakes need not always be corrected. If a child is stuck on a word, ask them to try and sound it out and then blend it together again, or model this yourself. For example "wish" w-i-sh "wish".

READING CORNER PHONICS covers two grades of synthetic phonics teaching, with three levels at each grade. Each level has a certain number of words per story, indicated by the number of bars on the spine of the book:

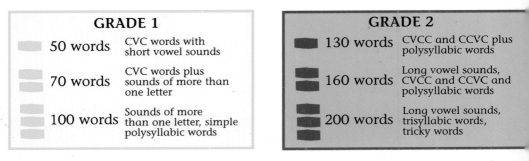

GRADE 1	
50 words	CVC words with short vowel sounds
70 words	CVC words plus sounds of more than one letter
100 words	Sounds of more than one letter, simple polysyllabic words

GRADE 2	
130 words	CVCC and CCVC plus polysyllabic words
160 words	Long vowel sounds, CVCC and CCVC and polysyllabic words
200 words	Long vowel sounds, trisyllabic words, tricky words